HIP-HOP

50 Cent

Hal Marcovitz

Mason Crest Publishers

50 Cent

FRONTIS Bestselling rapper 50 Cent, who has sold more than 10 million albums since emerging on the hip-hop scene in 2003, poses for a publicity photo.

PRODUCED BY 21ST CENTURY PUBLISHING AND COMMUNICATIONS, INC.

MASON CREST PUBLISHERS INC.
370 Reed Road
Broomall, Pennsylvania 19008
(866)MCP-BOOK (toll free)
www.masoncrest.com

Printed in Malaysia.

9 8 7 6 5 4 3 2

Library of Congress Cataloging-in-Publication Data

Marcovitz, Hal.
    50 Cent / Hal Marcovitz.
      p. cm. — (Hip-hop)
    Includes bibliographical references and index.
  ISBN-13: 978-1-4222-0110-7
  ISBN-10: 1-4222-0110-4
  1. 50 Cent (Musician)—Juvenile literature. 2. Rap musicians—United States—
Biography—Juvenile literature. I. Title. II. Series.
  ML3930.A13M37 2007
  782.421649092—dc22
  [B]   2006017324

Contents

Hip-Hop Timeline

1974 Hip-hop pioneer Afrika Bambaataa organizes the Universal Zulu Nation.

1988 *Yo! MTV Raps* premieres on MTV.

1970s Hip-hop as a cultural movement begins in the Bronx, New York City.

1985 *Krush Groove*, a hip-hop film about Def Jam Recordings, is released featuring Run-D.M.C., Kurtis Blow, LL Cool J, and the Beastie Boys.

1970s DJ Kool Herc pioneers the use of breaks, isolations, and repeats using two turntables.

1979 The Sugarhill Gang's song "Rapper's Delight" is the first hip-hop single to go gold.

1986 Run-D.M.C. are the first rappers to appear on the cover of *Rolling Stone* magazine.

1970   1980   1988

1976 Grandmaster Flash & the Furious Five pioneer hip-hop MCing and freestyle battles.

1986 Beastie Boys' album *Licensed to Ill* is released and becomes the best-selling rap album of the 1980s.

1970s Break dancing emerges at parties and in public places in New York City.

1982 Afrika Bambaataa embarks on the first European hip-hop tour.

1988 Hip-hop music annual record sales reaches $100 million.

1970s Graffiti artist Vic pioneers tagging on subway trains in New York City.

1984 *Graffiti Rock*, the first hip-hop television program, premieres.

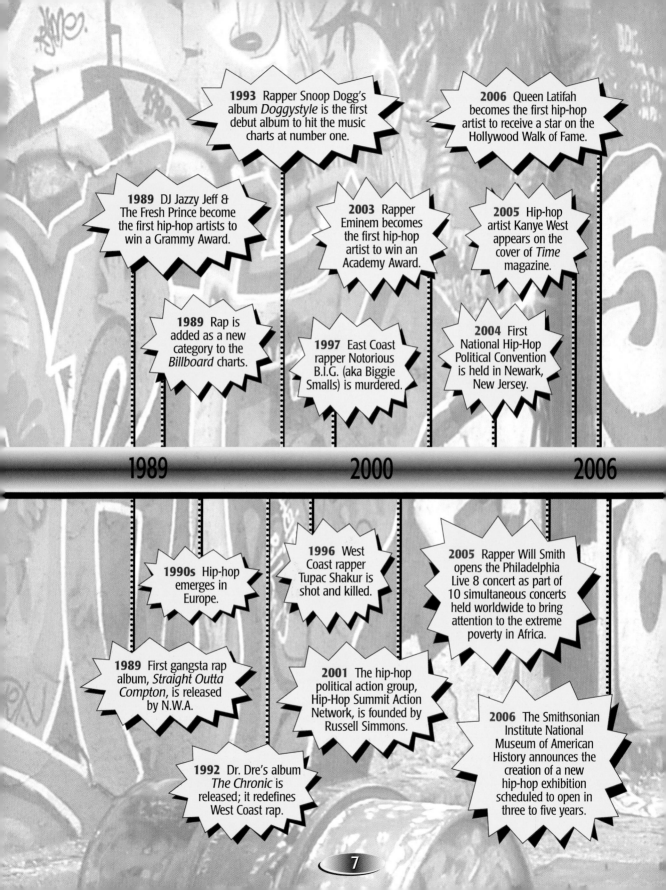

1993 Rapper Snoop Dogg's album *Doggystyle* is the first debut album to hit the music charts at number one.

2006 Queen Latifah becomes the first hip-hop artist to receive a star on the Hollywood Walk of Fame.

1989 DJ Jazzy Jeff & The Fresh Prince become the first hip-hop artists to win a Grammy Award.

2003 Rapper Eminem becomes the first hip-hop artist to win an Academy Award.

2005 Hip-hop artist Kanye West appears on the cover of *Time* magazine.

1989 Rap is added as a new category to the *Billboard* charts.

1997 East Coast rapper Notorious B.I.G. (aka Biggie Smalls) is murdered.

2004 First National Hip-Hop Political Convention is held in Newark, New Jersey.

1989   2000   2006

1990s Hip-hop emerges in Europe.

1996 West Coast rapper Tupac Shakur is shot and killed.

2005 Rapper Will Smith opens the Philadelphia Live 8 concert as part of 10 simultaneous concerts held worldwide to bring attention to the extreme poverty in Africa.

1989 First gangsta rap album, *Straight Outta Compton*, is released by N.W.A.

2001 The hip-hop political action group, Hip-Hop Summit Action Network, is founded by Russell Simmons.

1992 Dr. Dre's album *The Chronic* is released; it redefines West Coast rap.

2006 The Smithsonian Institute National Museum of American History announces the creation of a new hip-hop exhibition scheduled to open in three to five years.

Rapper 50 Cent performs at the World Music Awards ceremony in Monte Carlo, Monaco, in 2003. That year he won awards for Best Artist, Best Pop Male Artist, Best R&B Artist, Best Rap/Hip-Hop Artist, and Best New Artist.

1

Get Rich or Die Tryin'

I n 2003 the world was introduced to a new hip-hop star, 50 Cent. His debut album *Get Rich or Die Tryin'*, was an incredible success. The album went **gold** in its first week, spawned several hit singles (including the most popular song of the year, "In Da Club"), and eventually sold an amazing 6.5 million copies.

The hip-hop world had seen "gangstas" before—tough-talking poets of the streets who rapped about crime, guns, and drugs—but it had never seen a gangsta like 50 Cent. As a teenager, 50 dealt drugs and served time in prison. He headed a drug ring that moved thousands of dollars of **cocaine** a day. He is most often noted for having been shot nine times at nearly point-blank range—an incident he miraculously survived. On another occasion, an enemy tried to kill him by stabbing him in the stomach. He hadn't even known that he'd been stabbed until he was flee- ing the scene of the attack. When people heard 50 Cent rap about murder and revenge, there was no questioning his **veracity** because, in 50's case, his intensity came from his experience.

"Where I'm from, the price of life is cheap," 50 told *Rolling Stone* magazine in 2003. "For $5,000, you could kill somebody. You could pick a shooter. You could have a few different choices. Might do it for less than that if they like you." He was not exaggerating to impress the reporter. 50's criminal past was very real, the drugs he sold, very real, and the crime ring he had organized with other teens in his neighborhood, also very real.

A Star From Nowhere

In early 2003 very few rap fans had heard of 50 Cent. He had only a small and dedicated fan base on the streets of South Jamaica in Queens, New York, where he had grown up. At the time, all of 50's recorded music was contained on "mixtapes," homemade albums in which background music and beats borrowed from other records played below vocal tracks provided by the aspiring rapper. 50 Cent's mixtape albums sold briskly on street corners, in mom-and-pop record stores, and at New York City nightclubs where he performed. Still, he lacked a national record contract, and this meant his music reached relatively few fans.

Luckily for 50 Cent, his music caught the attention of Marshall "Eminem" Mathers, a rap superstar who had shaken the hip-hop world with his own best-selling albums, *The Slim Shady LP* and *The Marshall Mathers LP*. Eminem was one of the few white rappers to develop a real following, and his music spanned cultural gaps. Rather than rapping about women and money, he dealt with personal demons and anger—topics that many teens could identify with. Eminem had the attention of the masses, and they valued his opinion.

So when Eminem declared 50 Cent his favorite rapper in a radio interview a lot of hip-hop fans took notice. In 2002 Eminem featured three of 50's songs, "Wanksta," "Love Me," and "Places to Go" in the soundtrack for *8 Mile*, a semi-autobiographical film. In an interview with *Rolling Stone*, Eminem compared 50 to Notorious B.I.G. and Tupac Shakur, the late gangsta stars whose rhymes reflected the violent and drug-infested world in which they grew up. Said Eminem:

"One of the things that excited me about Tupac was even if he was rhymin' the simplest words in the world, you felt like he meant it and it came from his heart. That's the thing with 50. That same aura. That's been missing since we lost Pac and Biggie. The authenticity, the realness behind it."

Famed rapper Eminem and legendary music producer Dr. Dre flank 50 Cent at the 2004 Shady National Convention. Eminem discovered 50 Cent and convinced Dr. Dre to share the expense of signing him to a contract and producing his first album.

Getting Rich

Following the production of *8 Mile*, Eminem convinced his friend, fellow hip-hop **mogul** Dr. Dre, to help produce 50's first album, which would be titled *Get Rich or Die Tryin'*. The two rap stars signed 50 to a contract valued at more than $1 million—a huge sum to be paid to a relatively unknown rapper. Their labels, Aftermath Entertainment and Shady Records, marketed 50 Cent as an authentic gangsta, and by early 2003 hip-hop fans were anxiously awaiting 50 Cent's debut.

As with many hot albums, **bootleg** copies had been smuggled out of the studio after it was finished. Before the album was available in stores, the bootlegs were sold on the street and posted on the Internet

50 Cent shakes hands with Jimmy Iovine, the chairman of Interscope Records. Interscope promotes and distributes albums for Shady Records and Aftermath Entertainment, the labels that offered 50 Cent a $1 million bonus for his 2003 debut album.

and made available for downloading. A week before the record's distributor, Interscope, was prepared to release *Get Rich or Die Tryin'*, it had already been illegally downloaded some 300,000 times.

While most artists are upset about illegal file-sharing, 50 Cent credits the practice with making him a star. In an interview with *USA Today* he said, "I wouldn't exist as an artist without it. If you can create enough of a demand to be bootlegged before you have a deal, it is the greatest form of promotion."

Because of the illegal copies, Interscope had no choice but to move up the release date. In February 2003, during the first four days of the album's release, it sold 872,000 copies. Another 822,000 copies were sold the following week. The CD was so hot that record stores could not keep it on the shelves. After two months the album was certified six times platinum, meaning sales soared over 6 million copies.

Pure Gangsta

Music critics were quick to recognize that the album was something special. When 50 Cent raps about the hard life on the street, he has the

This image shows the cover of 50 Cent's first album, *Get Rich or Die Tryin'*. The bullet hole on the cover references the many times that 50 Cent has been shot. Marketing experts used his experiences to show audiences that he was a real gangsta.

street cred to back up his words. *People* magazine music critic Chuck Arnold said the album's "gritty delivery brings a rough-and-tumble realism to the hard-core beats, proving that 50 Cent is much more than chump change."

Get Rich or Die Tryin' was filled with themes that were very familiar to fans. For instance, the album included the single "Many Men (Wish Death)," which had the sounds of gunshots in the background. In the song, 50 raps:

Rapper 50 Cent performs at the Hot 97 Block Party at Nassau Coliseum on Long Island in 2003. Most music critics praised the songs on *Get Rich or Die Tryin'*, and it was the best-selling album of the year.

> **"Blood in my eye dawg and I can't see
> I'm trying to be what I'm destined to be
> And niggas trying to take my life away . . .
> My back on the wall, now you gon' see
> Better watch how you talk, when you talk about me
> 'Cause I'll come and take your life away . . ."**

Wrote *Rolling Stone* music critic Christian Hoard:

> **"Given his history of violence, the sense of impending doom on 'Many Men [Wish Death]' rings clearer than it would coming out of the mouth of any other rapper, save maybe Biggie and Tupac. Part of the reason he seems so credible, so really real, is because you actually believe 50's life may be in danger."**

But "Many Men (Wish Death)" wasn't the breakout hit of the album. That distinction went to "In Da Club," in which 50 Cent boasted about climbing out of the streets into the world of glitter. In the song he makes no secret of his intentions: "And the plan is to put the rap game in a choke hold . . . I'm feelin' focused man, my money on my mind . . . I got a mill out the deal and I'm still on the grind."

The title of the album, *Get Rich or Die Tryin'*, says it all: In 50 Cent's world, money is one of the few virtues, and the pursuit of it is worth any sacrifice. In such a world, a vice is whatever keeps the gangsta from his money. "This is how they think in the 'hood. This is my mind-set and these are the things that go on," 50 Cent wrote in his autobiography, *From Pieces to Weight*. "This is why I say the rhymes that I say."

Curtis James Jackson III borrowed his stage name 50 Cent from a man who had been renowned as a street thug during the 1980s. He felt the nickname would be an inside reference that other gangstas would understand.

2

From the Streets to Stardom

Curtis James Jackson III, also known as 50 Cent, was born amid the poverty and crime of South Jamaica, a depressed neighborhood in Queens, New York. Until he reached stardom, South Jamaica was the only world Curtis knew. Many hip-hop stars seek street cred by rapping about gunfights, dope deals, and police abuse, but Curtis lived those experiences.

He was born on July 6, 1975, to 15-year-old Sabrina Jackson. Curtis never knew his father, and Sabrina never talked about him. At first Sabrina and her baby made their home in her parents' crowded household. Sabrina was the youngest of nine children, and most of the Jackson children still lived at home. Eventually, though, she found her own apartment and supported herself by hustling drugs. She left Curtis where he was, to be raised by his grandparents. In his autobiography 50 Cent wrote:

> **"Every time I saw her, she would have something for me. Every visit was like Christmas. If there wasn't a toy, clothing, or a piece of jewelry, there was cold, hard cash. When I was six, she got me a children's dirt bike. . . . By that time, I began to pick up that she was selling drugs, so I knew she had probably taken it from someone who couldn't afford to pay what she wanted in cash. I didn't care. It actually made the bike seem more than it was because I knew she was thinking about me when she was working."**

When Curtis was eight years old, his mother was murdered during a drug deal. Curtis recalled that his grandfather cried when he broke the news to him. "Seeing my grandfather cry was like watching [a] horror [movie]," he later said. "I was like, that's not supposed to happen. . . . Even at eight years old, you know what it means when you hear your mother isn't coming back. It meant that Christmas was over."

Wild and Unpredictable

Following his mother's death, Curtis became a wild and unpredictable boy. He misbehaved in school, ignored his studies, and looked up to the men in the neighborhood who always seemed to have new and expensive things. Curtis knew they were drug dealers, but they were rich, and that was what mattered—he wanted that lifestyle for himself. When he reached the age of 11, he started selling cocaine. 50 wrote in his book:

> **"I was still in public school, so the only time I could hustle was after school hours, when my grandparents thought I was just playing games in the street. I picked it all up quick, because you can learn everything you need to know to hustle in under a year. . . . The more I did it, the easier it got."**

By the time he entered Andrew Jackson High School in Queens, Curtis had become a busy drug dealer on Guy R. Brewer Boulevard, the main strip that runs through South Jamaica. Prosperous drug dealers seldom manage to avoid notice by police, and Curtis was no exception. When he was 17 years old, he was arrested and given a drug test. He failed, and was sent to live in a drug rehabilitation facility.

In the movie *Get Rich or Die Tryin'*, Marc John Jefferies plays young Marcus, the character modeled after 50 Cent. In this scene Marcus is being scolded for misbehaving by his mother, played by Viola Davis.

He spent two uneventful years in the facility before he was released. As soon as he got out, though, he returned to Guy R. Brewer Boulevard to take up hustling again. He wrote, "I got the itch. I wanted to be back on the strip, selling crack, selling cocaine, selling whatever was moving. Like, not *now* but *RIGHT now*."

Everything he had been taught about drug prevention was quickly forgotten when he saw the kind of money his old friends were pulling in. Soon he recruited other young people from the neighborhood to work for him. Even though he was not even 20 years old, Curtis was running a ring that moved $5,000 worth of drugs a day.

Shock Treatment

Once again, the police caught up with Curtis. The second time he was arrested, he faced a prison sentence of nine years. However, because he was still a teenager, prosecutors offered him a deal: He could avoid prison if he enrolled in the New York State Department of Correctional Services Shock Incarceration Program. "Shock," as it was known, was essentially a **boot camp** in the woods of Beaver Dams, New York. Convicts spent six month "tours" in a military-style environment that included intense physical exertion, drilling, discipline, and hard work.

Curtis accepted the program and suffered through living outdoors in freezing weather, waking up before dawn, and performing a total

These mug shots were taken when Curtis was arrested for dealing drugs in 1994. Rather than go to jail, Jackson chose to attend a "boot camp" program meant to rehabilitate him. Once his sentence was finished, though, he returned to his criminal lifestyle.

of 650 hours of exhausting physical labor. "There were no razor-wired concrete walls, no sharpshooter-manned gun turrets, no dull gray steel bars—just woods," he wrote.

Curtis endured the boot camp, then returned to South Jamaica and the drug business. He re-established himself as a local dealer, but this time decided he would sell drugs only until he could find another way to make money. Soon after returning to Queens, Curtis's girlfriend, Tanisha, became pregnant. Curtis did not want to end up in jail with no way of supporting the child. He wrote:

> **"Tanisha really made me think long and hard about myself. She said that she didn't like the idea of having to raise a kid by herself if I would end up in jail, or worse. That's when I started to think about doing something besides selling drugs. I had a kid coming and I didn't want to raise my son or daughter in that world. And more important, I wanted to be there to be part of my child's life."**

In 1997 Tanisha gave birth to a baby boy, Marquise. Although Curtis and Tanisha never married, Curtis dedicated himself to being a good parent. He knew he would have to give up drug dealing or his son would grow up without a father.

Becoming a Rapper

Like many young people growing up on urban streets, Curtis was a fan of hip-hop music, particularly the gangsta rap that had been pioneered by the Compton, California, group N.W.A and the solo artists Notorious B.I.G. and Tupac Shakur. Occasionally Curtis and his friends created their own mixtapes. This was how Curtis found he had a talent for stringing together rhymes.

In 1996 a friend introduced Curtis to Jason Mizell, otherwise known as Jam Master Jay, a member of the group Run-D.M.C., one of "old-school" rap's most successful acts. Curtis convinced Jam Master Jay to listen to some of his mixtapes, and the rap veteran was immediately impressed with what he heard. The tapes were rough and amateurish, but with the right guidance, Curtis had the talent to become a star. Jam Master Jay signed the rapper to a contract, which gave him access to a studio where he could hone his skill. Jam

50 Cent is pictured here with his nine-year-old son, Marquise Jackson, as they attend the *Child Magazine* 2006 fashion show in New York City. The birth of Marquise made Curtis consider changing his lifestyle.

Master Jay also made it clear that Curtis would have to give up drug dealing. 50 Cent wrote in his book:

> "He said he didn't want that type of energy around him and wouldn't work with me if I was still in the streets. The reason he had taken me under his wing

was to give me an out from what I was doing. I respected where he was coming from. I didn't get into the drug game because I thought it was a cool thing to do. I got into it to make money and I didn't see any alternatives. If rapping was going to get me out of the 'hood, so be it. Just give me the beat and put me in the studio. **"**

Jam Master Jay taught Curtis how to organize rhymes and set them to a beat. Curtis created dozens of mixtapes, which he then used to make his own CDs—even creating the art for the album covers on his

Jason Mizell (Jam Master Jay) is on the right in this photo of the pioneering rap group Run-D.M.C. During the 1980s, Run-D.M.C. helped bring hip-hop music into the mainstream, and they were the first rappers to appear on the cover of Rolling Stone.

own. Mixtapes rarely sell more than a few hundred copies because sales depend on word of mouth. To combat this, rappers will try to get their CDs into the hands of influential radio disc jockeys, hoping they will play songs they like from the tapes on their radio programs.

This is what happened to Curtis. His self-produced albums were played on New York City radio stations, which boosted sales into the thousands. Through word-of-mouth he was becoming one of the hottest rappers in New York, even though he didn't have a record contract.

While producing his mixtapes, Curtis searched for a stage name. He settled on "50 Cent," a name once used by Kelvin Darnell Martin, a notorious drug dealer and thug who had been murdered in 1987. The short name would be easy to remember. And the memory of Martin lent a tough and sinister background to the name. "I just felt it was something an insider would get and the rest of the world would just think it was catchy," 50 wrote. "The real 50 Cent was a stickup kid . . . who used to rob rappers. He had passed, but he was respected on the streets, so I wanted to keep his name alive."

Sending the Wrong Message

In 1999, 50 Cent's popularity came to the attention of producers at Columbia Records. Columbia signed him to a record deal, and he went into the studio to record *Power of the Dollar*. While working on the album, 50 stumbled into a feud with rapper Jeffrey Atkins, who performs under the name Ja Rule.

Allegedly Ja Rule had been robbed, and one evening, in a New York City nightclub, he noticed 50 Cent talking to the man who he believed had robbed him. Ja Rule accused 50 of being a conspirator in the robbery, and the two men exchanged angry words. A few months later, when 50 Cent appeared at a nightclub in Atlanta, he found himself staying at the same hotel as Ja Rule. They confronted each other in a hallway and came to blows. The rivalry became a part of 50's music and helped push sales of his mixtapes long before an official album was released.

In May 2000, as Columbia was preparing to release *Power of the Dollar*, 50 Cent was shot while sitting in his car outside his grandmother's house. He sustained nine bullet wounds, including one shot that hit him in the mouth and knocked out one of his teeth. He survived the shooting, telling police that the assault may have been payback for a drug deal he had pulled years ago. Columbia Records,

Rapper and actor Ja Rule performs in Los Angeles, 2005. During the early days of 50 Cent's career, bad feelings developed between the rapper and Ja Rule. The feud may have been the reason for a 2000 brawl during which 50 Cent was stabbed.

sensitive to criticism that gangsta rap sent the wrong messages to listeners, abruptly shelved the album and cancelled its contract with 50 Cent. Once again without a record contract, 50 went back to producing mixtapes.

This time 50 Cent's tapes caught the attention of rapper and producer Eminem, who declared him an incredible talent and signed him to a record deal with his own record label, Shady Records, and with

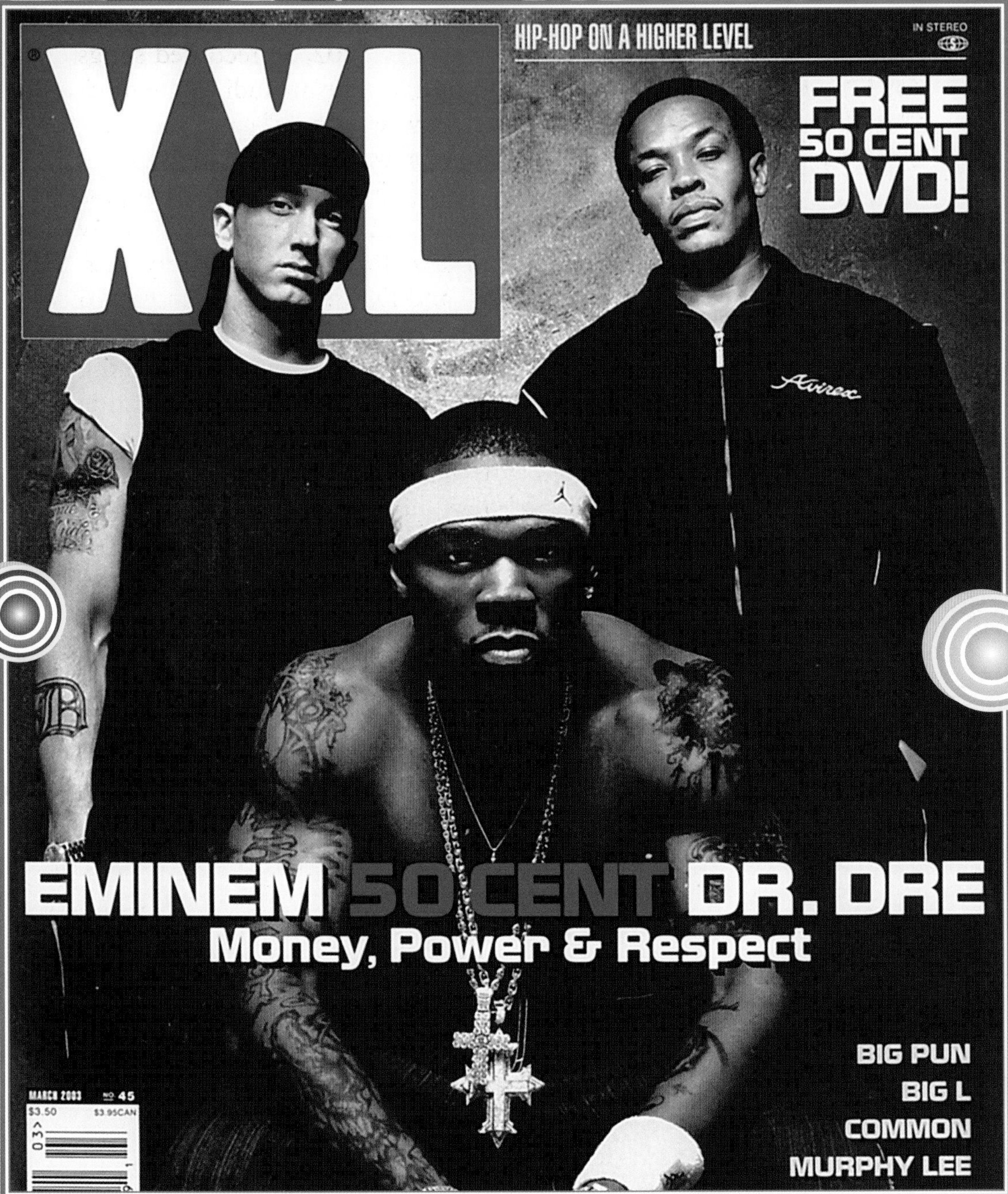

HIP-HOP ON A HIGHER LEVEL

IN STEREO

XXL

FREE 50 CENT DVD!

EMINEM 50 CENT DR. DRE
Money, Power & Respect

BIG PUN
BIG L
COMMON
MURPHY LEE

MARCH 2003   NO 45
$3.50 $3.95CAN
03>

The March 2003 issue of *XXL* magazine features Eminem and Dr. Dre standing behind their new star, 50 Cent. The title "Money, Power & Respect" sums up the attitude that 50 seeks to inject into his music.

Dr. Dre's label Aftermath Entertainment. In 2002, 50 recorded songs for Eminem's semi-autobiographical film, *8 Mile*, including the track "Wanksta," which was an attack on phony "would-be" gangstas. Most of 50 Cent's fans assumed that the insults were meant for Ja Rule.

50's feud with Ja Rule probably led to the second attempt on his life. Soon after the scuffle in Atlanta, 50 Cent was recording in a New York studio when the lights went out in the room. Suddenly men rushed in and started a brawl with 50 and his crew. "The fight was so quick I didn't even know what happened," he wrote. "They ran in, threw some sucker punches, and ran out. I wasn't sure what was going on, so I got out and hopped in a cab and went home." On the ride home, 50 discovered that he had been stabbed in the stomach, but the wound was minor. "A few hours later, my phone started ringing and people were telling me they heard that Ja Rule's crew had stabbed me in the studio," he said. "That's how I found out who it was." The stab wound was a shallow cut so minor that 50 Cent thought the whole incident was more of a publicity stunt than an attack.

Two years later, in 2002, Jam Master Jay was shot and killed in his recording studio. Police suspected that one of 50's enemies had killed Jam Master Jay for violating a **blacklist**. The police offered protection to 50, but he turned them down. He did, however, start wearing a bullet-proof vest whenever he went out in public.

50 Cent accepts his award as World Best Pop Male Artist during the World Music Awards ceremony in Monte Carlo. The rapper received many awards, thanks to his breakthrough 2003 debut album _Get Rich or Die Tryin'_.

3

Rap Superstar

Under the guidance of Dr. Dre and Eminem, 50 Cent's *Get Rich or Die Tryin'* became one of hip-hop's landmark albums. The success of *Get Rich or Die Tryin'* brought 50 Cent the wealth and fame he wanted. However, he still found it hard to escape from the gangsta lifestyle he had known since childhood.

Even though 50 Cent had stopped dealing drugs and had now dedicated himself to music, he could not escape minor scraps with the law. In early 2003 New York police found a gun in a car in which he was a passenger. The authorities dropped the charges after they determined that the gun was owned by one of the other passengers, who had been working as a bodyguard.

Then in early 2004 50 Cent allegedly assaulted a fan at a Massachusetts nightclub. 50 had been performing on stage when a fan threw water at him. "He removed his gold chain, handed it to someone on the stage next to him and jumped off the stage into the crowd," nightclub owner Michael J. Barrasso told the *Boston Herald*. The rapper's **entourage** followed him into the crowd. "I don't know who they were after," Barrasso said. "There was a lot of pushing and shoving."

50 pled no contest to an assault charge in the Massachusetts case. Judge Robert Kumor sentenced him to **probation** and said he would not send him to jail if he stayed out of trouble for the next two years. According to E! Online, Kumor warned 50 that he would do well to leave the gangsta life behind and start setting an example as a law-abiding citizen. "You're a cross-cultural entertainer," the judge said. "You have an obligation to people in society."

Grammy Voters Ignore 50

50 Cent had turned out to be a truly astonishing musical talent. Early in 2004 many critics expected him to win a Grammy Award for *Get Rich or Die Tryin'*. The Grammy Awards, sponsored by the National Academy of Recording Arts and Sciences, are the music industry's top honors. 50 was nominated for three Grammy Awards, including Best New Artist, Best Rap Male Performance, and Best Rap Song for "In Da Club." Wrote *Albany Times Union* music critic Greg Haymes, "50 Cent should change the title of his album to *Get Grammy or Die Tryin'*. It's in the bag . . . Can Grammy voters ignore the dominance of hip-hop any longer? Can they ignore the power of 50 Cent to sell a whopping 6.5 million CDs in yet another year of tumbling sales?"

Put simply: yes. In the two rap categories, 50 lost the awards to Eminem, who won for the soundtrack to his film, *8 Mile*. In the Best New Artist category, the Grammy was awarded to the rock group Evanescence. 50 did not take his loss well. As Evanescence singer Amy Lee started making her acceptance speech, 50 strode onto the stage in an act of defiance, drawing attention away from the winner. Grammy watchers were outraged. Wrote *NY Rock* columnist Jeanne Fury, "Dude, you lost. Swallow your pride. It's okay. You still gangsta. Even though you were completely shut out of awards."

Developing Talent

50 put the loss behind him and got on with his career, turning 2004 into a busy year. He started developing the talent of G-Unit, the group of rappers who accompanied him on stage and provided many of the vocal tracks for his album. To promote the group, 50 started his own label called G-Unit Records. Soon the label had produced albums for G-Unit members Christopher Lloyd, who raps under the name Lloyd

After losing the Best New Artist Grammy to rock group Evanescence, 50 Cent surprised the audience by going onto the stage in protest. The incident of poor sportsmanship earned him criticism from viewers and commentators, who felt he should have stayed in his seat.

Banks; David Darnell Brown, known to his fans as Young Buck; and rapper Marvin Bernard, whose stage name is Tony Yayo.

They were all young men from Queens, and 50 had known them since childhood. "When I got them in the studio, they were *green*. Yayo was rhyming with his back to the mike and Banks was screaming all over the place," 50 wrote in his autobiography. "They were so used to rhyming in the street that they had to be retrained for records."

Under 50's guidance G-Unit produced the album *Beg for Mercy*, which sold 2.3 million copies. Young Buck's album, *Straight Outta Ca$hville*, featured the hit single "Let Me In." And Tony Yayo's first solo

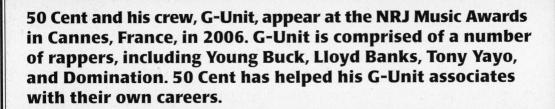

50 Cent and his crew, G-Unit, appear at the NRJ Music Awards in Cannes, France, in 2006. G-Unit is comprised of a number of rappers, including Young Buck, Lloyd Banks, Tony Yayo, and Domination. 50 Cent has helped his G-Unit associates with their own careers.

album, *Thoughts of a Predicate Felon*, debuted at number two on the *Billboard*'s 200 chart. Banks's solo album, *The Hunger for More*, debuted on the *Billboard* pop music chart in first place and sold nearly a million copies in its first month of release. Wrote *People* magazine music critic Chuck Arnold, "Banks's laid back, sometimes singsong delivery is reminiscent of 50, who executive-produced *Hunger* and raps on two cuts." He added that Banks "emerges as more than just 50 Cent's sidekick. He's a bankable talent in his own right."

Later G-Unit Records attracted rap stars from other hip-hop labels anxious to work with 50 Cent, including the rap duo Mobb Deep, comprised of Albert Johnson, also known as Prodigy, and Kejuan Muchita, also known as Havoc. Prodigy and Havoc were already successful recording artists when they left their label in 2006 to join G-Unit Records. Prodigy told the Associated Press, "These other companies we were working with, they just don't understand the music or what it takes to put it out there the right way. And hip-hop's not in their heart. It was just business. With G-Unit, it's deeper than that, son. It's for the love."

The partnership between 50 Cent and Mobb Deep produced the album *Blood Money*. The trio worked on the album for months, overseeing the development of some 40 tracks, although just 16 made the cut. "It was a joint creative process," Havoc told the Associated Press. "We trust 50's judgment, and he trusts ours. We never bumped heads when it came down to picking songs because everything that he picked was in the Mobb Deep vein."

50 Cent's popularity has led to endorsement deals with many companies, such as Reebok. The rapper has endorsed a line of designer footwear for the shoe manufacturer. Here, he shows a sneaker to the media outside a New York nightclub.

50 Cent takes direction from veteran film director Jim Sheridan on the set of *Get Rich or Die Tryin'*. Although not exactly a biography, the film attempted to capture the essence of the rapper's rise to stardom.

Gettin' Rich

As 50 Cent found his popularity soaring, he became much more than just a rap star and producer; he was a brand. He signed a contract with shoe company Reebok to promote a line of sneakers and boots. While Reebok may have recognized that hip-hop is popular and will sell products, they were not entirely willing to accept that 50 Cent could be a poor role model. In Britain, Reebok pulled its 50 Cent ad because viewers complained that it glorified violence. And yet, that is precisely

While recording vocal parts for his video game, _Bulletproof_, 50 Cent takes a break for a photo. In addition to the rapper's voice, the game also includes many exclusive rap tracks from 50 Cent and other G-Unit rappers.

what made 50 Cent a popular, attractive spokesperson to begin with. Says David Kiley of *Businessweek*:

> **Advertisers have to decide if they are going to play in this space or not. If you want to leverage hip-hop, then there are no half-measures . . . And if Bill O'Reilly or Focus on the Family come knockin' at your door with boycotts, you are going to have to choose sides. Trying to play both the hip-hop street and the avenue of political correctness is not going to work.**

The rapper also sold a recording of his voice to a ringtone company and inked a deal with Sierra Entertainment and Vivendi Universal Games to produce a video game titled *Bulletproof*. Beverage company Glaceau even produced a grape-flavored drink and named it "Formula 50" after the rap star agreed to endorse the product. 50 also licensed a line of clothes under the name "G-Unit." In an article on recording stars, the *New York Times* said:

> **The stars-turned-marketers range from Britney Spears . . . to Lil Jon . . . but few have out-hustled 50 Cent, the Queens-bred rap star who has been striking deals with the urgency recommended so starkly in the title of his debut CD, *Get Rich or Die Tryin'*. Sources close to the artist say 50 Cent's forays into fashion, entertainment and even beverages in the last 12 months or so generated income in the $50 million range.**

50 Cent takes direction from veteran film director Jim Sheridan on the set of *Get Rich or Die Tryin'*. Although not exactly a biography, the film attempted to capture the essence of the rapper's rise to stardom.

4

Putting the Fear Behind Him

As he worked on his second album, 50 Cent was also putting his life on the big screen in the movie *Get Rich or Die Tryin'*. He plays the central character, Marcus. "I guess you can say [the film] *Get Rich or Die Tryin'* is a collage of my life," he said in an interview.

The film was directed by the Irish director Jim Sheridan, a six-time Academy Award nominee known for the films *My Left Foot* and *In America*. At the age of 56, Sheridan might seem like an unlikely director to helm a project about a rising hip-hop star, but he had grown up in a depressed area of Dublin, Ireland, and had once lived in a tough New York City neighborhood in the 1980s. He saw how crime and crack cocaine domi-nated the community. He also admitted to being a fan of hip-hop music. "I love rap music. I loved it from the beginning," Sheridan told a reporter for the *Buffalo News*.

50 Cent had performed on stage and in music videos, but he had no real acting experience—a fact that worried the producers of the film. They

suggested to Sheridan that he hire an acting coach to work with the rapper, but the director declined. Sheridan said that 50 Cent would essentially be playing himself in the film, which would require no special talent. "I thought, if I can't get a truthful performance out of this guy, just as he is now, I have no business being a director anyway."

The film opened to mixed reviews. Critics enjoyed the story and the action but, despite Sheridan's influence on 50's performance, they gave lukewarm praise to 50's acting abilities. *Entertainment Weekly* film critic Lisa Schwarzbaum wrote, "Not raised to let the softness out . . . and not at ease with the free exchange of facial expressions, the centerpiece of the show looks exposed and vulnerable on screen, and not in a good way."

Film reviewer MaryAnn Johanson also felt that the movie failed to get across its supposed message:

> **"Perhaps it's not so much the universal tale that Sheridan and screenwriter Terence Winter (a multiple award winner for his *Sopranos* scripts) seem to think it is. Sure, maybe everyone wants to get rich, but plenty folks . . . see no great virtue or drama in the 'die tryin'' part. . . . Everyone involved, behind and before the camera, assures us that the film is about how a life of crime is no way to make a living. So why does it feel like it's saying that a rapper ain't the real thing if he doesn't stray from the straight and narrow?"**

Ticket sales were also somewhat disappointing. The movie earned $45 million at the box office, including overseas sales, but considering that it cost $40 million to produce, there wasn't much profit for the movie company. Evidently 50's fans went to see the movie, but the rapper failed to expand his appeal beyond his core audience. Still, the film proved that 50 has a dedicated base of fans and the potential to become a much larger film star. Following the release of *Get Rich or Die Tryin'*, the rapper received additional film offers and has current productions underway.

The Murder Inc. Trial

As *Get Rich or Die Tryin'* opened in theaters, many eyes were on a much different story—one that was unfolding in a courtroom in New York

This scene from *Get Rich or Die Tryin'* shows Marcus (50 Cent) sitting in a cell. Most critics found that 50's acting ability left something to be desired. His voiceovers sounded vacant, and they felt his acting did not show emotional depth.

Murder Inc. executive Irv Gotti (formerly Irving Lorenzo), and rapper Ja Rule exit the Brooklyn Federal Court on November 30, 2005. Gotti and his brother Christopher were on trial for money laundering. Both were acquitted.

City. In 2005 a three-year federal investigation into the activities of the record label known as Murder Inc. resulted in the arrests of label president Irv Gotti and his brother, Christopher. The Gottis borrowed the name of their label from of an organization that had been established by New York City gangsters in the 1930s to take over their enemies' **rackets**.

Prosecutors alleged that the Gottis had used $1 million in profits earned by an illegal drug ring to produce hip-hop records. The money was said to have come from Kenneth "Supreme" McGriff, a notorious drug kingpin who had served 10 years in prison. During the trial witnesses testified that McGriff was additionally behind the 2000 attempted murder of 50 Cent because of the song "Ghetto Qur'an," which chronicled McGriff's violent rise to the top of drug dealing in Queens. According to the song:

> **" See niggas feared Prince and respected Preme**
> **For all you slow muthaf---as I'm a break it down iller**
> **See Preme was a businessman and Prince was the killer "**

Jon Ragin, a former McGriff associate, told prosecutors that McGriff and two other men, Robert "Son" Lyons and Chauncey "God B" Millner, fired at 50 while he sat in the car outside his grandparents' house. Ragin said he met with McGriff and the others in a New York City garage shortly after the shooting. According to the *New York Daily News*, Ragin told prosecutors, "Supreme said, 'I got him.' I didn't know who it was 'he got,' and Supreme explained that he got 50 Cent . . . He thought [50 Cent] was dead. He got shot so many times at close range and there was so much blood." In addition to this testimony, there were pager records which suggested that McGriff was plotting 50's murder.

McGriff faced other accusations as well. According to court records, federal investigators believed McGriff might also have been behind the murder of Jam Master Jay. Investigators suggested that back in 2000 McGriff wanted to scuttle 50 Cent's career just as it was taking off. According to the *New York Daily News*, the court records said, "Law enforcement agents are investigating the possibility that Mizell was murdered for defying the blacklist of 50 Cent."

Ultimately, the evidence offered by Ragin and the court records that connected the murder of Jam Master Jay to McGriff was kept out of the Murder Inc. trial. The judge in the trial ruled that the accusations had nothing to do with the Gottis' use of drug money to **underwrite** the production of hip-hop music. Therefore the jury did not hear that portion of evidence. The trial resulted in an **acquittal**. McGriff was never charged with the murder of Jam Master Jay or the attempted murder of 50 Cent, but he was soon charged with the murder of Queens rapper Eric "E Money Bags" Smith and drug dealer Troy

Singleton. Smith supposedly shot one of McGriff's associates, who later died. Prosecutors charge that McGriff had Smith followed and murdered in a drive-by shooting in an act of revenge.

By mid-2006 McGriff was awaiting trial in the case. The evidence concerning 50 Cent and Jam Master Jay that was suppressed in the money laundering trial will appear in the murder trial. If convicted for murder, McGriff could face the death penalty.

50 Cent found it in his best interests to stay far away from the Murder Inc. trial. The attention from the justice department meant that he no longer had anything to fear from McGriff or from Ja Rule, who had signed a record deal with Murder Inc. In his autobiography, he wrote, "I leave them alone now because they're not relevant. They'll never hurt anybody themselves."

50's Secret Weapon

While working on the film version of *Get Rich or Die Tryin'*, 50 also managed to spend some time in the studio with G-Unit and work on his follow-up album, which was titled *The Massacre*. The record was released in the spring of 2005. Critics welcomed 50 Cent's effort to branch out from pure gangsta rap.

50 had realized that there was more to life on the streets than gunfights, drug deals, and murder. People who live in South Jamaica, Harlem, Compton, and other high-crime areas feel the same emotions as everyone else. They have fun, feel pain, enjoy parties, and worry about their children. 50 Cent maintained his commitment to be true to the sounds and beats of the inner city streets, but with *The Massacre*, the rap star also intended to tell other stories with his music. In his autobiography 50 wrote:

> **"I knew I had to make different music; I had to have the whole range of emotion in my music to be taken seriously. I had to be happy, upset, funny, everything. Everyone knew I could be angry, but I had to let people hear me sound as if I didn't have a care in the world. I couldn't pretend like I was Angry Man all the time. That's not reality. In the course of one day, the average person is going to go through different emotions. As an artist, I had to change emotionally in my work so people could really enjoy my music**

as they changed. When someone's feeling happy, I should have a happy song for them; when he's pissed off, I should have a song for that, too."

On *The Massacre* 50 included some party tracks intended for the dance floor, a few romantic ballads, and even some comedy—he rapped about how G-Unit was helping to make him rich. Wrote *Rolling Stone* music critic Nathan Brackett:

50 Cent's second album, *The Massacre*, was released in 2005. Although generally not considered as good as *Get Rich or Die Tryin'*, *The Massacre* did reach number one on both the American and British charts.

50 Cent performs a medley of "Disco Inferno," "Outta Control," and "So Seductive" during the 2005 MTV Video Music Awards. The track "Outta Control" from *The Massacre* was remixed and re-released as a single in late 2005.

"50 almost never lets you see him sweat—he wants you to believe he could be doing something else, like being a drug kingpin; rhyming is just something he happens to be good at. Don't believe him: He works to vary his flow on *Massacre*, faking a muddy Southern drawl on 'This is 50,' assuming a soft, confidential tone on 'Ryder Music,' going for a dry bark on 'I Don't Need 'Em' . . . As always, 50's secret weapon is his singing voice—the deceptively amateur-sounding tenor croon that he deploys on almost every chorus here. 50 knows perfectly the limitations of his voice— he stays within his register and more than makes up in personality what he lacks in technique."

Fans responded enthusiastically to *The Massacre*. In April 2005 singles from the album held 4 of the top 10 places on the sales charts. The last recording stars to accomplish a similar feat were the Beatles, who did it in 1964.

Wearing a G-Unit shirt, 50 Cent performs at the NRJ Music Awards in Cannes, France. While the rapper says he is still focused on making music, he has also branched out into other areas of entertainment. In 2006, he filmed his second movie.

5

Rapping into the Future

Although *The Massacre* was an overwhelming hit among 50 Cent's fans, the rapper was once again shut out at the Grammy Awards show. 50 received three nominations for Grammy Awards in 2006, but the honors went to the Black Eyed Peas and rapper Kanye West. Again, 50 Cent harbored some ill feelings. He fumed to MTV News:

> "He puts together witty phrases and he's a great talent as a producer, but I still don't know who Kanye West is when I listen to him. I feel like Kanye West is successful because of me. After 50 Cent, [hip-hop fans] was looking for something non-confrontational, and they went after the first thing that came along."

Though he was disappointed, the bad feelings did not run deep enough to start a feud. Instead 50 focused his attention on another rapper—one he had originally taken under his wing. For months 50 had been feuding with Jayceon Taylor, also called The Game. Taylor was among the rappers who had joined G-Unit. According to press reports, The Game failed to support 50 in his various feuds with other rappers, and this disloyalty was more than 50 would allow. 50 also didn't believe The Game gave him proper credit for producing some of the tracks on his critically acclaimed debut album *The Documentary*, so he kicked him out of G-Unit.

The feud quickly became violent. On February 28, 2006, Kevin Reed, a member of The Game's Black Wall Street crew, was shot in the leg outside a radio station where 50 Cent was giving an interview. Hours later, shots were reported fired outside the building where 50's management company, Violator, maintained offices.

50 Cent and The Game decided to call a truce before the feud became fatal. To show their fellowship, the two each donated money to the Boys Choir of Harlem—50 presented the group with a check for $150,000, while The Game donated $103,500. 50 Cent said, "We're here today to show that people can rise above the most difficult circumstances and together we can put negativity behind us." The rap stars also made donations to the Compton Unified School District music program, which supports music education at schools in Compton, California, the city that spawned gangsta rap.

Charitable Works

During the press conference with The Game, 50 said he also planned to launch a new charity, the GUnity Foundation. Among 50's other charitable endeavors are his provision of college scholarships to students who attend his old high school, Campus Magnet High School, and his support of efforts to combat childhood **obesity**.

For most of his life, 50 Cent battled obesity. "I had all of the unhealthy habits," he told the Associated Press. "Soda . . . a lot of fast food, all those things." Since changing his habits and taking up exercise, 50 has developed a physique that he's proud of. His album covers show off his trim, well-muscled body.

To help battle childhood obesity, 50 agreed to serve as spokesman for a national competition among student chefs who are challenged to create nutritious school cafeteria recipes. The winner of the competition receives a $100,000 college scholarship. He also endorses Glaceau's Formula 50 Vitamin Water as a healthy replacement for soda.

Rappers 50 Cent and The Game hold up checks showing donations that they were making to the Harlem Boys' Choir in March 2005. The two used the charitable gesture as a way to show the public that they had put their feud behind them.

Violence and Rap

Soon after 50's beef with The Game was settled, violence once again shook the hip-hop world when rapper Deshaun "Proof" Holton was killed during an exchange of gunfire in a Michigan nightclub on April 11, 2006. Following Proof's death, reporters asked 50 Cent whether he thought gangsta rap is too violent. 50 agreed that the lyrics are often violent, but he also suggested that parents have a responsibility to teach their children that music is nothing more than entertainment.

"I think that the violence that happened to Proof and the violence that's happening across America right now has nothing to do with hip-hop. It has something to do with the people—the state of them—and the music doesn't alter that."

Deshaun "Proof" Holton (left) performs with Mekhi Phifer and Eminem in 2002. The April 2006 murder of Proof caused some people to examine the link between violence and hip-hop. 50 Cent, for one, believes the music does not cause or endorse violence.

Seemingly unable to escape discussions about violence, 50 Cent found himself involved in another very important social issue: whether the United States should continue waging the war in Iraq. In 2006—three years after the American invasion that toppled dictator Saddam Hussein—the country remained unstable. In Iraq members of the **insurgency** continued to wage guerilla warfare on American troops as well as ordinary Iraqi citizens. The war had grown increasingly unpopular, and many people were calling for the withdrawal of American forces. The issue was in the news nearly every day.

In the spring of 2006, 50 Cent traveled to Morocco to shoot scenes for his new film *Home of the Brave*. The film, with an expected release date of 2007, will tell the story of three soldiers who come home from the war in Iraq to find their attitudes about the war vastly changed. It is expected to be the first film to chronicle the war and its effect on American soldiers. In an interview with the *Morocco Times*, 50 said:

> **"The film is showing the effects of war. That's what's exciting to me about it, because it is totally relevant to what's going on right now. It shows not just what happens to a person after killing, but what happens when there is a lot of death around you. How your spirit changes."**

50 hopes his role in *Home of the Brave* will help soften his image. He had hoped that by turning to serious dramatic acting, he would be regarded as much more than just a gangsta rapper. In an interview with VH1, 50 said:

> **"The misperception is that I'm gangsta 50. . . . I *can* be [that] to people. I have a reputation. My past is my shadow; it follows me everywhere I go. All those things come from when I have no choice. They put my back against the wall, I gotta do what I gotta do."**

No Apologies for His Life

In the space of just six years, 50 Cent had gone from drug dealer to underground MC to international stardom. After exploding onto the scene as a major star of hip-hop, he continued to expand his skill set by

50 Cent pauses at the 59th International Cannes Film Festival in May 2006, where a few minutes of his film *Home of the Brave* were being previewed. The movie, directed by Irwin Winkler, is about soldiers returning home from the war in Iraq.

acting in movies, and even made a brief appearance on *The Simpsons*. In 2005, 50 took a step into the literary world when he published his autobiography, *From Pieces to Weight*. In telling his own story, 50 uses the tough and gritty language of the streets and holds nothing back. He makes no apologies for his life and hopes that the story of his success can inspire others. In his book 50 wrote:

This frame from *The Simpsons* shows the cartoon version of 50 Cent standing behind juvenile bad boy Bart Simpson. The rapper appeared in an episode called "Pranksta Rap," in which Bart feigns kidnapping to avoid being punished for attending a 50 Cent concert.

> "I am truly blessed. And I remind myself every day that if I'm in a good space now, it's because I been in a bad space for so long before. I don't consider myself a role model, because I think a role model should be speaking and saying something positive all the time.

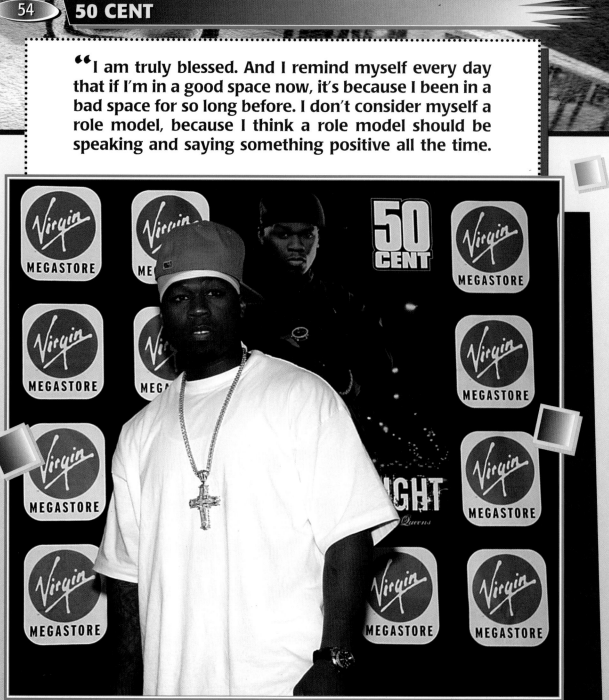

In August 2005 50 Cent met fans at the Virgin Megastore in New York, where he signed copies of his autobiography *From Pieces to Weight: Once upon a Time in Southside Queens*. More than 300 fans participated in the rapper's first book signing.

That ain't me. But my story has to be an inspiration to people that's from the bottom, people that's from the same walks of life I'm from. I'm proof that success is possible. They can look at me and say, I know *I* could do *this*, because *he* did *that*."

As for another album, 50 said that while he expects to be rapping into the future, for now his plans are up in the air. "My next album I don't know [when it'll come out]," he told MTV News.

"I want to see what they do if I sit down for a minute. When I say 'sit down,' I don't mean I won't be active—I'll leave the U.S. for a little while. I'll go outside the country and start developing my base outside the country a little more while they think I'm at home chillin'—then I'll come back and finish them off."

1975 Curtis James Jackson III born on July 6 in South Jamaica, Queens.

1983 Curtis's mother Sabrina Jackson murdered in a drug deal.

1986 Curtis begins dealing drugs.

1991 He drops out of high school to sell drugs full time.

1992 He is arrested for drug possession and sentenced to two years in a residential rehabilitation program.

1994 Arrested for drug dealing; sentenced to six months in a military-style outdoors boot camp.

1996 Meets Jam Master Jay, who teaches him to rap and demands that he give up drug dealing.

2000 50 Cent signs a contract with Columbia Records to record *Power of the Dollar* but loses the contract when he is shot and wounded.

2002 He records three songs for the soundtrack to Eminem's film *8 Mile*.

2003 50 Cent releases *Get Rich or Die Tryin'*, which becomes wildly successful and spawns three hit singles.

2004 He is arrested for assault in a Massachusetts nightclub. He pleads guilty and is placed on probation.

2005 50 Cent plays the lead role in the film version of *Get Rich or Die Tryin'* and releases *The Massacre*.

2006 He films the Iraq War drama *Home of the Brave*.

Mixtapes

2002 *Guess Who's Back*
No Mercy, No Fear

Solo Albums

2000 *Power of the Dollar* (unreleased)

2003 *Get Rich or Die Tryin'*

2005 *The Massacre*
Get Rich or Die Tryin' (film soundtrack)

Albums with G-Unit

2002 *God's Plan*

2003 *Beg for Mercy*

Films

2005 *Get Rich or Die Tryin'*

2007 *Home of the Brave* (anticipated release)

Awards Won

2003 Winner, BET Awards for Best New Artist and Best Male Hip-Hop Artist

Winner, MTV Video Music Awards for Best Rap Video and Best New Artist and nominated, MTV Video Music Awards for Video of the Year, Best Male Video, and Viewer's Choice

Winner, World Music Awards for Best Artist, Best Pop Male Artist, Best R&B Artist, Best Rap/Hip-Hop Artist, and Best New Artist

Winner, *Source* Awards for Album of the Year for *Get Rich or Die Tryin'*, Breakthrough Artist of the Year, and Single of the Year, "In Da Club"

Winner, American Music Awards for Favorite Hip-Hop Album for *Get Rich or Die Tryin'* and Favorite Rap/Hip-Hop Male Artist and nominated for American Music Awards for Fan's Choice Award

Winner, *Vibe* Awards for Artist of the Year, Dopest Album and Hottest Hook for "In Da Club"

Named Best New Artist by readers of *Rolling Stone*

2004 Nominated for Grammy Awards for Best Rap Performance by a Duo or Group with Lil' Kim; Best Rap Solo Performance for "In Da Club"; Best Rap Album for *Get Rich or Die Tryin'*; Best New Artist, and Best Rap Songwriter for "In Da Club"

2004 Winner, Brit Award for Best International Breakthrough Artist

2005 Winner, American Music Award for Favorite Rap/Hip-Hop Album for *The Massacre* and nominated for Favorite Rap/Hip-Hop Artist, Favorite Pop/Rock Male Artist, and Artist of the Year

2006 Nominated for Grammy Awards for Best Rap Solo Performance for "Disco Inferno"; Best Rap Performance by a Duo or Group with Eminem and Dr. Dre for "Encore" and with The Game for "Hate It or Love It"; Best Rap Song for "Candy Shop" and "Hate It or Love It"; and Best Rap Album for *The Massacre*

50 Cent. *From Pieces to Weight: Once Upon a Time in Southside Queens.* New York: Pocket Books, 2005.

Arnold, Chuck. "*Get Rich or Die Tryin'*". *People Weekly* vol. 59, no. 8 (March 3, 2003): p. 36.

———. "Lloyd Banks." *People Weekly* vol. 62, no. 6 (Aug. 9, 2004): p. 40.

Binelli, Mark. "No. 1 with a Bullet." *Rolling Stone* no. 915 (Feb. 6, 2003): p. 31.

Brackett, Nathan. "*The Massacre.*" *Rolling Stone* no. 969 (March 10, 2005): p. 107.

Brown, Ethan. "The Life of a Hunted Man." *Rolling Stone* no. 919 (April 3, 2003): p. 44.

———. *Queens Reigns Supreme: Fat City, 50 Cent and the Rise of the Hip-Hop Hustler.* New York: Anchor Books, 2005.

Brown, Jake. *50 Cent: No Holds Barred.* Phoenix, Ariz.: Colossus Books, 2005.

Haymes, Greg. "The Grammy-Go-Round: This Year's Awards Won't be Dominated by a Single Music Star." *Albany Times Union* (Feb. 8, 2004): p. I-1.

Heuer, Max, and Robin Washington. "Melee at Springfield Club as Irate 50 Cent Hops . . . Into Da Crowd." *Boston Herald* (May 10, 2004): p. 3.

Hoard, Christian. "The Realest." *Rolling Stone* no. 917 (March 6, 2003): p. 68.

Johnson, Brett. "Mobb Deep Rolls with a New Crew for New Album." Associated Press, May 8, 2006.

Jones, Steve. "G-Unit: That and 50 Cent Will Get You a Deal; 3 Hot Hip-Hop Artists Go Solo." *USA Today* (Aug. 3, 2004): p. D-1.

Lawson, Terry. "Loose Change: Acclaimed Director Fought to Keep Film True to Rapper's Story." *Buffalo News* (Nov. 11, 2005): p. G-5.

Leeds, Jeff. "$50 Million for 50 Cent." *New York Times* (Dec. 26, 2004): p. 2-2.

Marzulli, John. "Hit Team Kept Filling Fitty with Lead. Bombshell Testimony Rocks Trial of Rap Bigs." *New York Daily News* (Nov. 22, 2005): p. 7.

Parker, Eric. "50 Cent Connection." *Rolling Stone* no. 911 (Dec. 12, 2002): p. 18.

Ro, Ronin. *Raising Hell: The Reign, Ruin, and Redemption of Run-D.M.C. and Jam Master Jay.* New York: Amistad, 2005.

Schwarzbaum, Lisa. "Common Cent." *Entertainment Weekly* no. 850 (Nov. 18, 2005): p. 101.

Internet Resources

http://www.50cent.com

50 Cent's official Web site includes a biography of the rapper, interviews with 50, and news updates on his activities.

http://www.aftermath-entertainment.com/

The Web site for Dr. Dre's Aftermath Entertainment includes interviews with some of rap's top stars, including 50 Cent, Eminem, and The Game.

http://www.getrichordietryinmovie.com/main.html

Official Web site for the film *Get Rich or Die Tryin'* features interviews with 50 Cent, director Jim Sheridan, and other principal figures in the production.

http://www.vh1.com/artists/az/50_cent/artist.jhtml

VH1's official artist profile contains biography and discography information. There are also video clips and fan message boards.

acquittal—verdict of not guilty in a criminal trial.

blacklist—a list of people who are to be punished or boycotted. To be blacklisted is to be added to such a list.

boot camp—physically exhausting camp experience usually employed by the military to train new recruits. This approach is also used to rehabilitate criminals.

bootleg—unauthorized copy of a recording in which the artist and producer do not receive financial compensation.

cocaine—illegal drug drawn from the leaves of the coca plant, grown mostly in the mountains of Colombia.

entourage—group of friends or employees who regularly stay with a person; 50 Cent's entourage includes his bodyguards.

gold—record industry designation for an album that sells over 500,000 copies.

insurgency—members of an organized group opposed to a ruling body; they often resort to violence and terrorism to topple a government.

mogul—a powerful person, particularly in business.

obesity—unhealthy weight problem often attributed to a person's improper nutrition.

probation—status granted to a criminal defendant that permits him freedom provded that he follow rules of good behavior.

rackets—illegal activities organized and controlled by a group of criminals.

underwrite—to provide financial support so that a business venture may occur; in return, the backers expect to be compensated with a share of the profits.

veracity—the truth or accuracy of a statement or claim.

Hal Marcovitz is a journalist who has written more than 70 books for young readers as well as the satirical novel *Painting the White House.* His other biographies in the HIP-HOP series include *Notorious B.I.G.*, *Tupac Shakur,* and *Dr. Dre.* He lives in Chalfont, Pennsylvania, with his wife, Gail, and daughters Ashley and Michelle.

Picture Credits

page